DONKEY and CARLO

DONKEY
and
CARLO

by Elaine Raphael and Don Bolognese

Harper & Row, Publishers
New York, Hagerstown, San Francisco, London

DONKEY and CARLO
Copyright © 1978 by Elaine Raphael and Don Bolognese

FIRST EDITION

Library of Congress Cataloging in Publication Data
Raphael, Elaine.
  Donkey and Carlo.

  SUMMARY: Carlo becomes so involved at the market that he forgets his promise to Donkey.
  [1. Donkeys—Fiction.   2. Friendship—Fiction]
I. Bolognese, Don, joint author.   II. Title.
PZ7.R1812Do   [E]   77-25660
ISBN 0-06-020552-0
ISBN 0-06-020553-9 lib. bdg.

For Annie and Elise

Carlo and Donkey lived on a farm outside town. Every morning Carlo and Donkey worked together in their garden.

"Ahh. See how big the artichokes are today?"
Carlo said as he sprinkled water on them. Donkey nodded as he carried the water for Carlo.

"What beautiful carrots." Carlo gave one to
Donkey to taste. Donkey munched with delight.

"Have you ever smelled such sweet basil?"
Carlo asked. Donkey smelled the basil and nib-
bled on a few leaves. He gave Carlo a big smile.

"Everything is growing so well. I think they are
ready for market," said Carlo as he turned up
the earth around the carrots. Donkey nodded his
head and went about his work.

They worked all day raking, digging and pulling up the weeds. When the sun was down past the pear tree they knew it was time to rest. Carlo went to sleep dreaming of market day. Donkey lay down. He switched his tail and watched the bees fly over his zinnias. A rabbit hopped through the garden. Donkey waited for the stars to come out. Finally he fell asleep with his nose nestled in the parsley patch.

The next day, very early in the morning, Carlo
went to the garden alone. He worked while Donkey was sleeping. He worked while the sun was
rising behind the hill. The woodpeckers were
just peeping their heads out of their nest.

"To market. To market," Carlo sang softly. He cut the artichokes and the cabbages and put them in baskets. He cut the roses too. The sun reached the parsley patch and the light warmed Donkey's nose. He woke up rubbing his eyes.

"To market. To market," Carlo sang louder. Donkey's ears went up in surprise. He looked around the garden. Carlo was picking the basil and marigolds.

"We are going to market," said Carlo when he saw Donkey standing in the garden. And he hurried past him to pick some zinnias. Donkey stamped his feet. He showed his long white teeth. And then sat down in the middle of the garden. Carlo stopped working. He put his basket of flowers down.

"Please, Donkey, don't be stubborn now. I need your help. The vegetables are too big. The flowers are too many for me to carry alone." Donkey didn't move.

"Please come to town," Carlo pleaded. And he rubbed Donkey's nose. He scratched Donkey's ears. He pinched his cheeks and rubbed his nose again.

"You are such a good friend, Donkey. I promise we will be home before dark," Carlo said.

Finally Donkey nodded. And soon they were on their way to town.

The sun was high overhead when they reached
town. The marketplace was crowded. But Carlo
and Donkey found a tiny spot next to a man
selling pots and pans.

"Isn't this wonderful?" Carlo said. Donkey
looked and sniffed. There were too many people.
The houses were too close together. He couldn't

even smell his basil. Donkey sat down. Carlo put
out all the vegetables and flowers.

Soon people stopped and looked. Then they
bought. At last only one bunch of basil was left.
Donkey grinned from ear to ear. Soon he would
be home again. Carlo sold the last bunch.

"See, Donkey, that didn't take long. Now we will go home. But first I must buy some cakes." He went to the cake stall. Donkey waited while Carlo ate a cake, then another and another. Donkey pulled at Carlo's sleeve.

"Just one more, please, Donkey, a plum cake." Carlo bit into a plum cake while Donkey pulled him away.

"Yes, yes, Donkey. We are going home now." Carlo patted Donkey's head.

In the center of the square a band was playing.
"I know that song," Carlo shouted, and he
began singing. And he sang the next song and
the next. Donkey sat down. His ears back, his
eyes closed. He wanted to go home. Finally the
singing stopped. Donkey looked up. Now Carlo

was following a parade. Donkey jumped up and
ran after him. He tugged at Carlo's coat.

"Donkey, Donkey, don't worry! We will go

home soon. This is only a short parade." Donkey
followed Carlo and the parade around the square.
The parade passed in front of a group of per-
formers. Carlo stopped to watch a juggler tossing
rings in the air.

"Look, Donkey," Carlo said, "five rings at one time." Carlo watched the juggler for a long time. And Donkey waited.

The sun disappeared behind the town steeple. Evening shadows filled the square. The merchants and the shoppers went home.

The square was empty except for Carlo, Donkey and the juggler.

The juggler packed up his rings and bowed. Carlo gave him a coin. Donkey yawned.

"Oh, Donkey, you are tired too," Carlo said, rubbing his eyes.

"I think it is too late to go home. We will stay in town tonight and leave in the morning." Donkey didn't look at Carlo.

"Come, Donkey, follow me. I will find us a place to sleep."

Carlo found a small stable. It had one tiny window high in the rafters. Pigeons flew in and out to their nest. In the corner a mouse was eating a piece of bread.

Carlo was so tired that he quickly fell fast asleep in the hay. The pigeons cooed as they snuggled to rest. The mouse curled up in the corner to sleep. Only Donkey couldn't close his eyes. He thought of home. He thought of his zinnias and his pear tree. He pulled at Carlo's coat sleeve. Carlo answered with a snore. He pulled at Carlo's scarf. Carlo snored louder. Donkey looked up at the tiny window. He couldn't see the stars. He could see only a small piece of sky. The moon's light barely touched the window's edge. Donkey rested his head in the hay. The hay didn't smell like his parsley patch.

"*HEEEE HAWWWWWW,*" he brayed as loud
as he could. "*HEEEEEE HAWWWWWWWWW.*"

Carlo sat up, startled.

"What is it? What is wrong?"

Donkey brayed louder. Carlo tried to pat Donkey on the nose. But Donkey brayed and flicked
his ears.

"Are you hungry? Do you want some pie?"
Carlo said, looking in his pocket. Donkey turned
his head away.

"What is it, my Donkey?" Carlo said. "Please
tell me."

Donkey looked at Carlo. His eyes were very
sad. Then he lowered his head until it touched
his feet.

Carlo thought for a while. Then he put on his hat.

"Donkey, I have not been a good friend. And this morning you were such a good friend to me. I didn't keep my word to you, my Donkey. I am sorry." Carlo put his arms around Donkey. "Let's go home now," he whispered in Donkey's ear.

They left the stable. They passed through the
town gate. And by the moon's light found their
way home.

The sun was coming up when Donkey and Carlo reached their farm. They sat down to an early breakfast of carrots and plum cake. Then Carlo fell asleep right where he was sitting. But Donkey had to sleep with his nose in the parsley patch.